EXTRAORDINARY
WARREN'S
WORLD

EXTRAORDINARY WARREN'S WORLD

Previously published as two separate books, titled
Extraordinary Warren and *Extraordinary Warren Saves the Day*

by Sarah Dillard

ALADDIN

New York   London   Toronto   Sydney   New Delhi

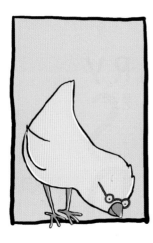

This book is a work of fiction. Any references to historical events, real people, or real places are used fictitiously. Other names, characters, places, and events are products of the author's imagination, and any resemblance to actual events or places or persons, living or dead, is entirely coincidental.

🪔 ALADDIN
An imprint of Simon & Schuster Children's Publishing Division
1230 Avenue of the Americas, New York, NY 10020
First Aladdin edition June 2020
Copyright © 2014 by Sarah Dillard
All rights reserved, including the right of reproduction in whole or in part in any form.
ALADDIN is a trademark of Simon & Schuster, Inc., and related logo is a registered trademark of Simon & Schuster, Inc.
For information about special discounts for bulk purchases, please contact Simon & Schuster Special Sales at 1-866-506-1949 or business@simonandschuster.com.
The Simon & Schuster Speakers Bureau can bring authors to your live event.
For more information or to book an event contact the Simon & Schuster Speakers Bureau at 1-866-248-3049 or visit our website at www.simonspeakers.com.
The text of this book was set in Carnes Handscript and Jacoby.
The illustrations for this book were rendered digitally.
Manufactured in China 0420 SCP
10 9 8 7 6 5 4 3 2 1
Library of Congress Control Number 2019948052
ISBN 978-1-5344-6347-9 (hc)
ISBN 978-1-5344-6346-2 (pbk)
ISBN 978-1-5344-7563-2 (eBook)
This book was previously published as two separate books, titled
Extraordinary Warren and *Extraordinary Warren Saves the Day*.

CHAPTER 1

Once there was a chicken.

Just an ordinary, average,
run-of-the-mill chicken.

He lived in a little barnyard
on a quiet farm.

His name was Warren.

Warren was not the only chicken
on the farm. There were lots of others.

They spent their days pecking for
chicken feed. They pecked all day long.

EVERY SINGLE DAY.

It made Warren . . .

DIZZY.

The chickens stopped pecking.
They looked at one another.
And laughed.

They didn't understand Warren.

He felt very alone.

CHAPTER 2

Warren wasn't the only one who was unhappy.

Millard the rat
was also looking for
something different.

But day in, day out,
all he found was junk.

It made Millard . . .

CRANKY!

At that moment, Warren walked by.

He couldn't believe his ears.

As Millard dreamed of better meals to come . . .

Warren rushed home
to share his news.

Warren was as cheerful as he had ever been.
There was just one problem.

CHAPTER 3

When Millard awoke from his nap, he couldn't believe his eyes. Or his luck. A chicken AND an egg.

How extraordinary!

He climbed on top of the trash can and,
to his delight, saw even more chickens!

Meanwhile, back at the barnyard,
Coach Stanley had big plans for the flock.

PHWEET!

You chicks peck
and peep all day
long. It's time
you started
acting like birds.

It's time you
learned to fly.

Warren heard the whistle and Coach Stanley's announcement.

He got to thinking.

Did you hear that, Egg? If I'm going to be Chicken Supreme, I probably should learn how to fly.

Right?

Bye-bye, Egg. Next time you see me, I'll be in the air.

Warren raced to the farm, making his way to the front of the class.

Coach Stanley made flying look easy.

The chicks lined up to take their turns.

Warren was the last to go.

Warren's hopes
and dreams
were dashed.

He was so
upset, he couldn't
even face Egg.

CHAPTER 4

At the trash can, Millard was busy planning himself a feast.

41

As Millard left, Warren noticed the book he was carrying.

And then he realized . . .

Sure enough, Warren saw that the chickens were about to walk into trouble . . .

and into Millard.

Warren told the
chicks Millard's REAL
plans.

But no one believed him.

They were too excited about the barbecue.

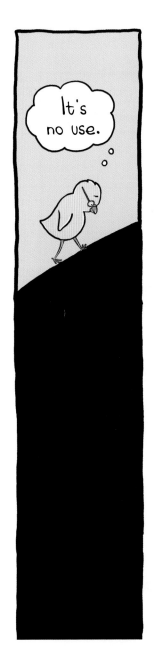

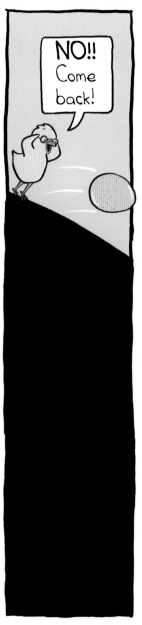

49

CHAPTER 5

Without even thinking, Warren . . .

FLAPPED!

JUMPED!

I'll save you, Egg!

And *flew!*

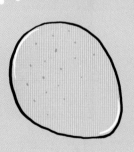

Millard was almost ready for his barbecue.

The table
was set.

The grill was
ready to light.

He was waiting for the main course to
arrive, when all of a sudden . . .

Slowly, Millard sat up.
He was furious when he saw the mess!

My grill is destroyed!

The barbecue is OFF!

As soon as Millard stormed away . . .

...the chickens arrived.

CHAPTER 6

But not all the chickens had left.
Warren felt a tap, tap on his back.

He turned around.

59

The two feathered friends headed home,
walking and talking.

Warren and Egg stopped in their tracks.

And off they went. . . .

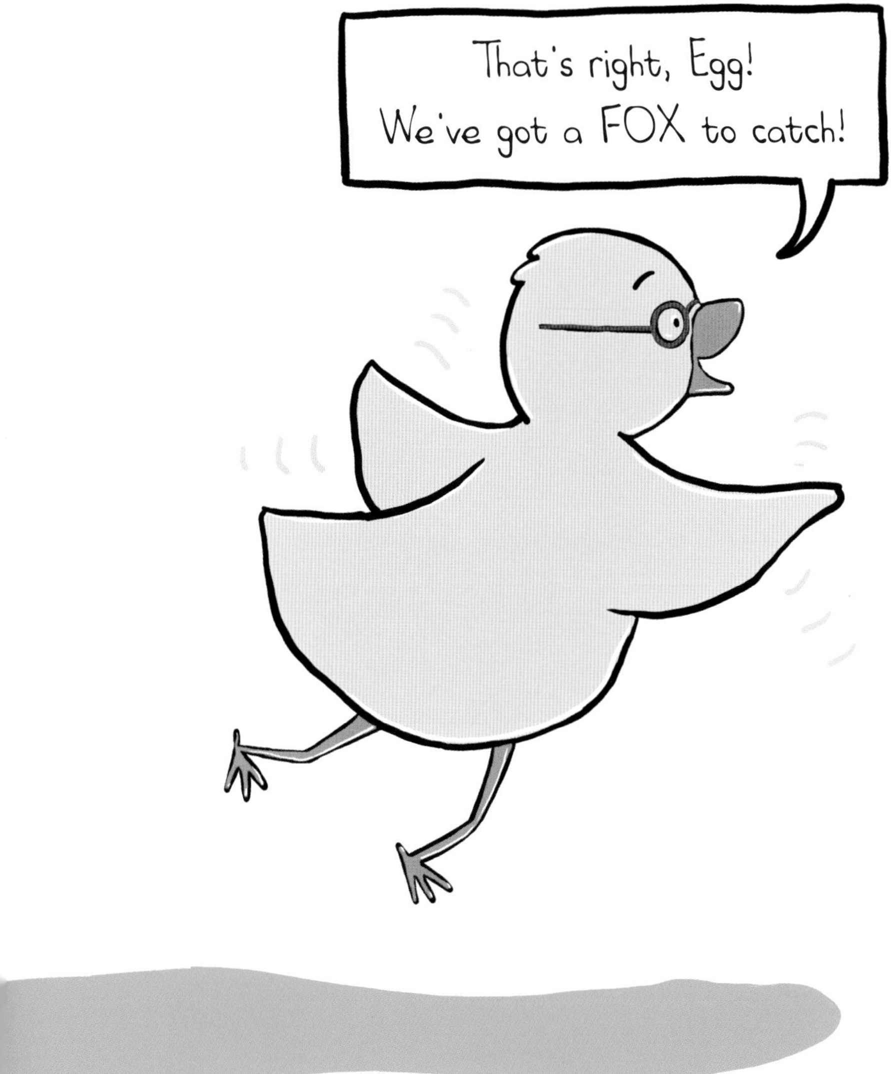
That's right, Egg! We've got a FOX to catch!

CHAPTER

After out-foxing the fox, it was back to
the same everyday routine of . . .

THUD

pecking and peeping,
peeping and pecking.

But then Coach Stanley made a few changes
to their daily routine.

From sunup until sundown, the chicks
were busy.

They danced.

They stretched.

They sang.

Warren liked all the new activities.
He especially enjoyed nap time.

He dreamed of all the
faraway places he
would visit someday.

Warren's naps never lasted long enough.

All the chicks thought Warren was hilarious.

No one took Warren seriously, except for...

CHAPTER 8

Egg.

Warren answered Egg's endless questions.

Warren taught Egg everything he knew.

☆Listen to Coach. ☆Never trust a rat.

☆The early bird catches the worm.

☆The moon is made of green cheese.

☆Look to the brightest star.

☆If at first you don't succeed,

try, try again.

That night, while the other chickens slept,

Egg thought
about flying,

and Warren
thought about
the moon.

CHAPTER 9

The next morning, Egg woke up before everyone else.

He was determined to fly.

That didn't work.

Egg tried and he tried.

One more time
he jumped,

flapped, and . . .

flew!

He landed on the other side of the road.

Off Egg went.

First he found . . .

Then he discovered . . .

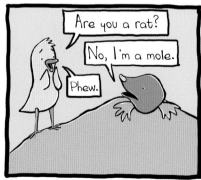

Egg kept exploring until he was
in the middle of . . .

But when Egg turned to leave,
he wasn't sure which way to go.

CHAPTER 10

When Warren woke up, he was still thinking about the moon. He thought about it all day.

At breakfast.

At exercise class.

At nap time.

During gymnastics, he told the chicks his plans.

But after lunch, during their weekly
game of hide-and-seek, Warren was all business.

It was finally his turn to be "IT."

Warren found everyone,
except for . . .

He had forgotten all about
Egg!

Warren searched high and low,
inside and out,
and all around the farm.

But Egg was
nowhere to be
found.

That left one last
place to look.

Millard's trash can.

Warren ran all the way to the side of the road.
Then he stopped.

Warren knew he had no choice.

He looked to the left. He looked to the right. And . . .

CHAPTER 11

On the other side of the road, Warren spotted a cow.

He raced away as fast as he could,

past the pond

and the molehill,

deep into the cornfield,

until he was out of breath.

And then he
remembered.

CHAPTER

Back at the barnyard, the chickens were singing the last song of the day.

The chicks scurried to
find Coach Stanley.

Immediately, the chicks started decorating.

They made so much noise, they woke up . . .

MILLARD.

Warren looked high and low, but Egg was nowhere to be found.

It was getting dark, and a little bit cold, and he wasn't sure what to do next.

But then Warren heard a familiar voice.

Egg—that's it!

And there's the star! Let's go!

Warren and Egg followed the light of
the star across the road and home,

just as Millard was crossing
in the other direction.

CHAPTER

When Warren and Egg reached the farm,
the search party was in full swing.

Egg told everyone about their adventures.

The chicks thought Egg was hilarious.

They laughed all the way to bed.

But Warren and Egg
weren't quite ready
to go to sleep.

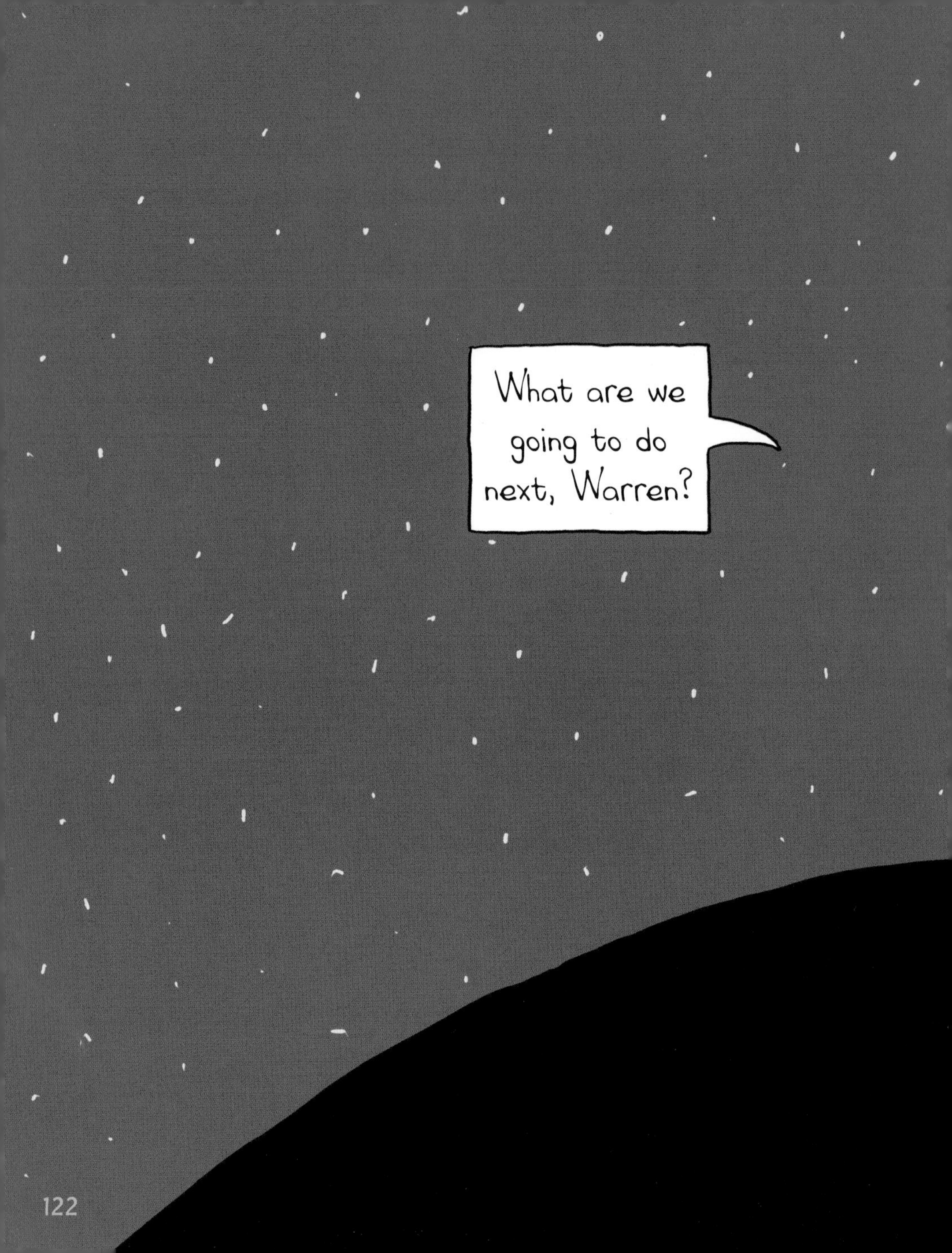
What are we going to do next, Warren?

Meanwhile, on the other
side of the road . . .

MoOOOVe it!

Sarah Dillard grew up in a small town in Massachusetts. She studied art and English literature at Wheaton College, and illustration at the Rhode Island School of Design. She lives on a mountain in Vermont with her husband and dog, both of whom inspire many of her characters and ensure that she goes for a walk every day. You can visit Sarah online at sarahdillard.com.

HELP SNAIL

LEAVE HIS BUCKET AND FIND A FOREVER HOME

in these two funny stories, together
in one graphic novel chapter book!